Katie Kazoo, SWITCHEROO

Horsing Around

by Nancy Krulik • illus   Wendy

Grosset & Dunlap

For Jeff and Amy—N.K.

Whoa! For our blue-ribbon pal, Kate R.—J&W

GROSSET & DUNLAP
Published by the Penguin Group
Penguin Group (USA) Inc., 375 Hudson Street, New York, New York 10014, USA
Penguin Group (Canada), 90 Eglinton Avenue East, Suite 700,
Toronto, Ontario M4P 2Y3, Canada
(a division of Pearson Penguin Canada Inc.)
Penguin Books Ltd., 80 Strand, London WC2R 0RL, England
Penguin Group Ireland, 25 St. Stephen's Green, Dublin 2, Ireland
(a division of Penguin Books Ltd.)
Penguin Group (Australia), 250 Camberwell Road, Camberwell, Victoria 3124, Australia
(a division of Pearson Australia Group Pty. Ltd.)
Penguin Books India Pvt. Ltd., 11 Community Centre, Panchsheel Park, New Delhi—
110 017, India
Penguin Group (NZ), 67 Apollo Drive, Rosedale, North Shore 0632, New Zealand
(a division of Pearson New Zealand Ltd.)
Penguin Books (South Africa) (Pty.) Ltd., 24 Sturdee Avenue,
Rosebank, Johannesburg 2196, South Africa

Penguin Books Ltd., Registered Offices: 80 Strand, London WC2R 0RL, England

Library of Congress Cataloging-in-Publication Data is available.

ISBN 978-0-448-44677-6   10 9 8 7 6

Chapter 1

"Okay, dudes, it's time for us to turn over a new leaf," Mr. Guthrie said as he greeted class 4A early Monday morning.

Katie Carew started giggling the minute she saw her teacher. Mr. Guthrie was wearing brown shoes, brown pants, and a brown long-sleeved shirt. He had red, yellow, and brown leaves taped all over his arms and chest. He looked just like a fall tree—if fall trees wore glasses and had ponytails.

The Mr. G. tree totally fit in with the 4A classroom today. The whole room looked like a forest. There were colorful construction-paper leaves taped to the floor and construction-paper trees on the walls. Small stuffed animal squirrels and chipmunks were in the corner behind some leaves.

Katie put her backpack down and plopped into her beanbag. All of the kids in class 4A sat in beanbag chairs. Mr. G. thought kids learned better when they were comfortable.

"Let me guess. We're studying fall today," Kevin Camilleri said as he sat down.

"Oh, I'll get an A in that," George Brennan announced. He ran across the classroom, tripped over his shoelace, and fell face-first into his beanbag chair.

Katie giggled. She knew George had fallen down on purpose. George was always doing funny things like that.

"Maybe we'd better call this our *autumn* leaves learning adventure," Mr. G. suggested. "To avoid more accidents."

"So do we get to decorate our beanbags now?" Andy Epstein asked.

Katie was sure they would. Mr. G. let the

kids decorate their beanbag chairs *every* time they started a new learning adventure.

But today Mr. G. said, "Not yet. First you're going to decorate yourselves."

The kids all stared at their teacher. *What was he talking about?*

Mr. G. pulled a huge garbage bag out of the classroom closet. Katie and her friends ran to see what was inside.

"It's just a bag of old leaves," Kevin said. He sounded disappointed.

Katie understood why he felt that way. Mr. G.'s surprises were usually really wild. Like the day he had the class pretend to be birds and dig through chocolate mud for gummy worms.

Or the time he brought in an egg as the class pet. The kids had all figured there was some sort of bird inside. But instead, Slinky the class snake had popped out. Slinky was definitely the greatest—and weirdest—pet in the whole school.

And Katie would never forget when Mr. G.

wore a Japanese bathrobe to school and fed
them all green tea cakes for snack, just because
their class was Japan in the school Olympics.
Katie hadn't really liked the green cakes, but
she still thought it was cool that Mr. G. was
pretending they were in Japan.

Compared to all that, a bag of leaves wasn't
very interesting.

Mr. G. handed each kid a different leaf.

Katie's was shaped like a hand with three fingers. On it was a sticker that said SASSAFRAS.

"If you're going to be in this forest, you have to be a tree," Mr. G. told the kids. "And at this time of year, many trees have colorful leaves. I want you to find the other leaves of your tree and then tape them to your clothes."

One by one, the kids searched inside the garbage bag for the leaves that matched the one in their hand.

"I'm a maple," Andy told the class.

"I'm an oak," Mandy Banks shouted out.

"I'm a dogwood," Emma Weber said.

After Katie found the other sassafras leaves in the bag, she cut strips of brown and black construction paper and wove them in and out like a basket.

"It's an empty nest," she told Mr. G. as she taped the basket to her shoulder. "All the birds have flown south."

Mr. G. laughed. "Very creative, Katie," he complimented her.

"Hey, my yellow leaf just fell off," Emma Stavros complained.

"So did my orange one," Kevin added.

"That's what they're supposed to do," Kadeem Carter told them. "Why do you think they call this season fall?"

"Can anyone tell me why the leaves turn different colors in the fall?" Mr. G. asked his forest of human trees.

Katie smiled and raised her hand. She knew the answer to this one. Her grandmother had told her all about it during a trip to the mountains.

"How about you, Katie Kazoo?" Mr. G. used the way-cool nickname George had given her back in third grade.

"It's because the days are getting shorter, so there's less sun. Without sun, the trees make less chlorophyll. That's the stuff that makes the leaves green," Katie explained. "Without the green chlorophyll, you can see the other colors in the leaves."

"Good job," Mr. G. praised Katie.

"Hey, look at George!" Kevin exclaimed suddenly.

The whole class began to laugh. George had taped leaves to his head and his rear end.

"You look more like a turkey than a tree," Kadeem told him.

A big smile crossed George's face. It was George's joke-telling smile. Katie knew what that meant . . .

"Speaking of trees," George said. "Do you know what month trees are scared of?"

"No, what one?" Emma Weber asked.

"Sep-*timber*!" George told her.

Everyone in the class laughed. Everyone but Kadeem, that is. He was thinking up a joke of his own to tell.

"How do trees get on the Internet?" Kadeem asked.

"How?" Andrew piped up.

"They *log* on!" Kadeem answered. He laughed really hard at his own joke.

"Cool! We've got a tree joke-off going on," Mr. G. exclaimed. "Your turn, George."

"Okay," George replied. He was up for the challenge. "What did the beaver say to the tree?"

"What?" Mr. G. asked.

"Nice *gnaw*ing you," George told him.

The class laughed even harder.

Katie looked around at all the other kid-trees in the forest-like classroom. Life in class 4A was definitely colorful. It was fun, too.

So much fun that Katie never wanted to *leaf*!

Chapter 2

"Go, Kevin! Go, Kevin!"

The kids at the lunch table were all cheering as Kevin popped another cherry tomato in his mouth. Kevin loved tomatoes more than anything. Today he was trying to break the cherry-tomato-eating record. He was up to sixteen already!

"Man, he's going to puke," Jeremy Fox said. "He just ate three tomatoes at once!"

"Go, Kevin! Go, Kevin! Go, Kevin!" The fourth-graders cheered even louder.

Kevin popped tomatoes seventeen, eighteen, and nineteen in his mouth and began to chew. Red tomato juice shot out of his mouth and across the table.

Now Mr. G. saw what was going on and put a stop to it. "Kevin, that's disgusting and you could choke," he scolded.

"Yes! Kevin, that's super-disgusting!" Suzanne Lock shouted at him. "You almost got tomato gunk all over my new cowboy boots."

Katie wasn't sure how tomato juice could have flown over the table and landed on her best friend's boots—which were *under* the table. She had a feeling Suzanne just wanted everyone in the fourth grade to notice she had new cowboy boots. That was kind of the way Suzanne worked.

"You got new boots?" Miriam Chan asked Suzanne.

"Let me see," Emma W. said.

Suzanne smiled. She had managed to take the attention away from Kevin.

"These boots are just like the ones cowboys wear when they ride horses," she said, sticking

out her feet. "Well, cow*girls*, anyway. See all the fancy jewels on the sides?"

"Those are really cool," Mandy said.

"Mega-cool," Jessica Haynes agreed.

"They're nice boots," Becky Stern said in her slow, southern accent. "But they're not the kind of boots I wear when *I* go horseback riding."

All the girls' attention switched to Becky.

"You go horseback riding?" Emma W. asked. "I always wanted to do that!"

Becky nodded. "I take lessons at the Cherrydale Stables."

"I thought you took gymnastics classes," Suzanne said in a not very nice tone.

"I do," Becky told Suzanne. "But now I take horseback riding, too. A person can take more than one kind of class."

Katie knew that was true. She took cooking classes at the community center. She also took art classes. And clarinet lessons, too.

"What kind of boots are for riding?" Zoe Canter asked Becky.

"They're black leather," Becky said. "And they go up to my knees. They're what you're supposed to wear when you ride English style. That's the kind of riding they teach at the Cherrydale Stables."

"Your boots sound sort of plain," Suzanne huffed.

Becky shrugged.

"Do you have a horse?" Katie asked excitedly.

Suzanne shot her a nasty look. Apparently she didn't like Katie talking to Becky about horseback riding.

But Katie didn't care. She loved animals. She wanted to hear all about this.

"I don't have my own horse," Becky admitted. "I ride a pony who lives at the stables. He's the sweetest pony in the whole world. He's chocolate brown and his name is Brownie."

"Brownie," Katie repeated. "I like that."

"Horseback riding is incredible," Becky told the kids at the table. "I love that feeling of going up and down, up and down, up and—"

"Becky, stop," Kevin said suddenly.

Katie looked over at him. His face had turned a weird greenish color.

"Oh, man," Kevin groaned. "I feel sick." He got up and ran from the table.

"I told you guys he was going to lose it," Jeremy said. "Too many tomatoes."

"You are always so sensible," Becky cooed to Jeremy. She batted her eyes. "You're the smartest boy in the whole grade."

Now it was Jeremy's turn to look like he was about to puke.

Katie felt bad for Jeremy. Everyone knew that Becky had a huge crush on him. They also knew that Jeremy did not have a huge crush on Becky—or even a tiny one!

"Um, Becky, is it hard to get up on a horse?" Katie asked, trying to turn Becky's attention away from Jeremy.

"Well, Brownie's a pony, so he's not as tall . . ." Becky stopped for a minute and thought. "You know, I have a picture of me sitting on Brownie's back. It's in my backpack. I'll go get it." She jumped up from the table and ran out of the cafeteria.

Jeremy sighed and rolled his eyes as she left. "I wish she would just ride off into the sunset like those old cowboys," he said. "Then I would never have to see her again."

Katie's eyes bulged. She couldn't believe what Jeremy had just said. "You do not wish that!" she exclaimed.

"Oh, yeah, I do, Katie Kazoo!" Jeremy assured her.

Katie frowned. She really, really wished Jeremy hadn't made that wish. Katie hated wishes. She had a good reason. She knew just how awful things could be when wishes came true.

Chapter 3

Katie was in third grade when she first got into trouble with wishes. It started one terrible, horrible day when Katie lost a football game for her team. Then she'd fallen in a big mud puddle and ruined her favorite pair of jeans. Even worse, she'd let out a huge burp in front of the whole class. How embarrassing!

That night, Katie had wished she could be anyone but herself. There must have been a shooting star overhead or something, because the next day the magic wind came.

The magic wind was a super-strong, tornado-like wind that blew only around

Katie. It was so powerful that every time it came, it turned Katie into someone else.

The first time the magic wind appeared, Katie turned into Speedy, the class 3A hamster. She'd escaped from her cage and wound up inside George's stinky sneaker. YUCK!

The magic wind came back again and again after that. It turned her into all kinds of people. Once it turned her into her grandfather! Katie had hair coming out of her nose and ears and her muscles ached all the time.

Another time the wind switcherooed Katie into Jeremy's kitten, Lucky. That time Katie had gotten into a fight with her own cocker spaniel, Pepper. He'd chased her right up a tree!

The magic wind followed Katie wherever she went—even all the way across the Atlantic Ocean! When Katie was in Italy on vacation, the wind turned her into a gondolier. She had to paddle a boat through the canals of Venice. Katie didn't know her way around the canals. She got a whole boatload of tourists lost. Katie didn't speak Italian. That made it hard to ask for directions!

Wishes could sure make life difficult. That was why Katie never made them anymore. But she couldn't tell Jeremy about the magic wind and switcheroos. He wouldn't believe her. Katie wouldn't have believed it, either, if it didn't keep happening to her.

So instead, she just said, "Why don't you go out to the yard for recess *now*, Jeremy?"

"I haven't eaten my dessert yet," Jeremy pointed out.

Katie shrugged. "What's more important? Green Jell-O or getting out of the cafeteria before Becky comes back?"

Jeremy didn't have to think about that at all. He just leaped up from the table and galloped out of the cafeteria.

Katie giggled. When it came to hiding from Becky Stern, Jeremy didn't horse around!

Chapter 4

That afternoon, Katie went to Suzanne's house for a playdate after band practice. When Suzanne opened the door, she was balancing a big basket of fruit on her head.

"What are you doing?" Katie wondered.

"I'm working on my posture," Suzanne explained. "My modeling teacher told me to walk around balancing a big book on my head. But that hurt. And besides, this is much more colorful."

Katie tried hard not to laugh. She knew Suzanne was taking this very seriously.

Suzanne reached up to the top of her head. "You want an apple?" she asked Katie.

Katie couldn't hold it in anymore. She started giggling.

For a minute, Suzanne looked surprised. But then she caught a glimpse of her reflection in the mirror. She started laughing, too.

Bam! The basket of fruit fell to the floor. An orange rolled under the couch.

Suzanne was crawling under the couch to get it when—

Ding-dong. The doorbell rang.

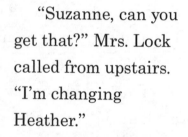

"Suzanne, can you get that?" Mrs. Lock called from upstairs. "I'm changing Heather."

Suzanne frowned. "I can't wait until that baby can change herself," she groaned as she stood up and peeked through the window to see who was at the door. "That's weird," she told Katie. "It's George."

That *was* weird. George and Suzanne were definitely not friends.

"George," Suzanne said as she opened the door. "Why are *you* here?"

Katie rolled her eyes. Suzanne could be so rude sometimes.

"I'm here to talk to your mom, not you," George answered.

Sometimes George could be pretty rude, too.

"Why?" Suzanne asked, without inviting George inside.

"It's about my new business," George said.

"What business?" Katie ran over to the door.

"Katie Kazoo, I didn't know you were here," George said. "Your house is next on my list."

"For what?" Katie wondered.

"My new leaf-raking business," he explained. He looked out at Suzanne's lawn. It was covered with dried, brown leaves. "You guys sure have a lot of leaves to rake."

"My dad's been busy," Suzanne told him. "He didn't have time to rake this weekend."

"That's why I'm here," George said. "I'll do it instead. *For a price*, of course."

Suzanne yawned. Katie figured she was bored with the conversation. After all, it wasn't about modeling, fashion, or herself.

"I'll get my mom," Suzanne said.

* * *

A few minutes later, George was busy raking up the leaves in the Locks' front yard. While Mrs. Lock made dinner, the girls played with Heather. They were dressing her up like she was going to a fancy party.

Suzanne got bored playing with her baby sister, but Katie loved it. Katie was an only child. She had no one to play with at home except Pepper. He could play fetch. And he could cuddle up with Katie when she watched TV.

But having a dog wasn't the same thing as having a little sister. Pepper never would have let the girls dress him up in a party dress and a hat. Actually, Heather didn't seem to enjoy it a whole lot, either.

"Heather, leave that hat on," Suzanne scolded her sister.

"No like!" Heather shouted back. She threw the hat at Suzanne.

Suzanne made a face. "You see what I mean, Katie?" she asked. "Heather does that all the time."

Just then George peeked his head into the house.

"Bye, Mrs. Lock," he shouted from the front door. "I'm done and I have to be home before six."

Uh-oh. Katie looked at the clock. It was 5:45. She was supposed to be home by six o'clock, too!

"I gotta go, Suzanne," she said, jumping to her feet.

"You're going to leave me alone with *her*?" Suzanne asked, pointing to Heather.

"Heather's not so bad," Katie replied.

"That's easy for you to say," Suzanne told her.

Katie picked up her clarinet and her book bag and opened the front door. But before she could even walk outside, Heather toddled past her into the front yard.

"Leaves!" Heather shouted. She ran as fast as her little legs could take her.

"Heather, get back here!" Suzanne shouted. She started to chase her sister.

BAM! A minute later, Suzanne and Heather had both pounced on the neat pile of leaves George had raked up. Yellow, brown, red, and orange leaves scattered everywhere.

"What are you doing?" George shouted angrily. He started running back. "I just raked those up."

Katie looked at George. He seemed really mad.

But not as mad as Mrs. Lock. She had just come outside. "Suzanne Elizabeth Lock!" she shouted.

Katie gulped. *Uh-oh.* Mrs. Lock had just used Suzanne's full name. When parents did that, it was never good.

"I cannot believe you just did that," Mrs. Lock continued. "George worked very hard."

"B-but Heather . . ." Suzanne began.

"Don't blame this on your little sister," Mrs. Lock warned. She scooped up Heather in her arms. "Help George rake up the rest of these leaves right now."

Katie looked at her best friend. Suzanne was angry now, too. Katie didn't blame her. None of this was really Suzanne's fault. It was

Heather's. But a baby couldn't help rake leaves.

Katie watched as Suzanne got an extra rake and began working with George. This sure wasn't going to make Suzanne like her little sister any better.

George wasn't too fond of Heather either at the moment. Katie wasn't sure which made him more angry—having to rake the leaves up again or having to rake them up with Suzanne.

Either way, George wasn't happy. And neither was Suzanne. Mrs. Lock had no idea what she'd just done. Making Suzanne and George rake leaves together was a recipe for disaster.

Which was why *Katie* was happy—to get going!

Chapter 5

Suzanne wasn't thinking about Heather or George when she got to school the next morning. She was too busy being annoyed with Becky Stern. Becky had worn her riding helmet to school. The girls were circled around her, admiring it.

Katie knew how much that must bug Suzanne. Suzanne was used to being the one in the middle of the circle. She was sure to say something to bring everyone's attention back to her.

"Becky, why are you wearing that?" Suzanne asked. "It's not like there are any horses on the playground."

"Everyone was so curious about my riding clothes, I thought I'd show them the helmet," Becky explained.

"*Everyone* wasn't curious," Suzanne told her. "I wasn't curious. Katie wasn't curious. *Jeremy* wasn't curious."

Katie scowled. Why was Suzanne dragging her into this?

But Becky wasn't upset about Suzanne mentioning Katie. She was more hurt that she'd mentioned Jeremy.

"Jeremy," Becky called across the playground. "Do you like my new riding helmet?"

Jeremy just rolled his eyes. Becky frowned. That obviously wasn't the reaction she was hoping for.

"They're never going to let you wear that thing in school," Suzanne continued. "And when you take it off, you'll have helmet hair."

Becky looked like she was going to cry. Especially when she took off her helmet and felt the top of her head. Sure enough, her hair was all flat.

"I hope Jeremy doesn't think I look ugly," she moaned.

At the moment Jeremy wasn't looking at Becky at all. He was on the other side of the playground. Far away from Becky.

Katie pulled Suzanne by the arm. "Why are

you being so mean?" she asked her.

"I'm not mean," Suzanne said. "I'm just sick of Becky being such a show-off."

Before Katie could say anything, a fight broke out on the other side of the playground!

"That was my idea!" Kadeem yelled. "I told you yesterday that my mom paid me a dollar to rake our lawn."

"Big deal," George screamed back. "That was for your mother. It doesn't count. I have a business. I rake leaves for lots of people. And I'm making a lot of money, too. In a few weeks I'll have saved up enough for a new skateboard."

"I'll bet I can earn more money than you can," Kadeem told George.

"Yeah, right," George huffed. "You're not the one with a leaf-raking business."

"I have one now," Kadeem insisted. "I'm starting right after school."

Katie looked around the yard and sighed. Things sure were a mess.

Suzanne was angry about not being the center of attention.

Becky was crying about her hair.

Jeremy was hiding from Becky.

And George and Kadeem were arguing.

Katie didn't know whether George or Kadeem was going to earn more money raking leaves. But one thing was a *sure* bet.

Trouble was definitely brewing in the fourth grade.

Chapter 6

"Pssst. Katie Kazoo, come here." Jeremy was hiding behind a tree when Katie arrived at school Wednesday morning. He was wearing dark sunglasses and a baseball hat.

"Jeremy, what are you . . . ?" Katie began.

"Shhh!" Jeremy shushed her. "I'm hiding from Becky."

"What did she do now?" Katie asked him.

"This is the worst thing *ever*," Jeremy told Katie. "She's in a horse show on Saturday *and she invited me*!"

Katie looked at Jeremy strangely. That didn't sound so bad.

"Just tell her you can't go," Katie suggested.

"I can't," Jeremy insisted. "That's the *really* bad part. She asked me in front of my *mother*."

"Oh." Now Katie understood.

"We were having dinner at Louie's Pizza Shop. Becky and her mom came in," Jeremy explained. "That's when Becky invited me to the horse show. And my mom said yes without even asking me first."

Katie frowned. "I hate when parents do that," she said.

"Now Becky is telling everyone I'm going to be her *special* guest." Jeremy groaned. "You gotta help me, Katie."

Poor Jeremy. Katie wished there was a way she could help him out. She always tried to be there for Jeremy when he needed her.

Be there for him . . . That was it!

"How about if I go with you?" Katie asked Jeremy. "And we can get some other kids to go, too. Then it will be a bunch of us. There won't be anything *special* about you being there."

Jeremy's face brightened. "Do you think other kids will come?" he asked hopefully.

A horse show sounded fun. But Katie wasn't so sure. Becky had been bragging a lot. People were getting kind of sick of that. Katie didn't say that out loud. She just said, "Let's hope so."

★ ★ ★

The first person Katie asked was Emma W. Emma was nice about it. She said she would try her hardest to come to the horse show.

"It's my big sister's turn to watch Matthew and the twins," Emma W. told Katie and Jeremy.

"Great!" Jeremy exclaimed excitedly.

"Thanks," Katie told Emma W.

Next Katie and Jeremy went over and asked Mandy, Emma S., Jessica, and Miriam to come to the horse show. Emma S. had a skating lesson, and Miriam had to go into the city with her parents. But Mandy and Jessica both promised to show up.

So far lots of girls were coming to the horse show. But Jeremy was the only boy. That still made him kind of special. And Katie didn't want that. She had to get some boys at the horse show as well.

"George, come here," Katie called across the playground.

George began walking toward Katie and Jeremy. He moved really slowly. His legs seemed stiff. And he was holding one of his arms.

"What's the matter with you?" Jeremy asked George.

"I raked a lot of leaves yesterday," George explained.

"You did a great job at our house," Jeremy assured him.

"Thanks," George answered. "After your lawn, I raked Mr. Brigandi's front *and* back yards."

Katie was impressed. Mr. Brigandi lived on her block. He had a lot of trees in his yard. That meant a lot of fallen leaves.

"No wonder you're sore," she said.

"Yeah, but I'm rich," George told her. "I'm going to earn more money than Kadeem. You'll see."

"Can you take a break from raking for a few hours on Saturday?" Katie asked George hopefully.

"To do what?" George asked.

"To come to Becky's horse show," Jeremy explained. "A whole bunch of us are going."

"*You're* going to Becky's horse show?" George asked Jeremy. He sounded surprised.

Jeremy groaned. "Don't ask."

"Please, George," Katie pleaded. "It'll be fun. We're trying to get a huge crowd."

"I'll come if Kadeem comes," George told her.

Now *that* was weird. Usually George stayed as far away from Kadeem as possible.

"Because I'm not going to give up an afternoon of raking lawns if he's not," George continued.

Oh. Now it made sense.

"I'll convince Kadeem to come," Jeremy said. "He owes me a favor. I helped him study spelling words last weekend."

"Then I'll be there, too," George assured him. "And I'll ask Kevin. He has karate in the morning, but maybe he can come after."

"Great!" Katie exclaimed. She smiled at Jeremy. "See? Everyone wants to help you."

Everyone except Suzanne, anyway.

"Why would I want to go to blechy Becky's horse show?" Suzanne asked Katie.

Katie sighed. Asking Suzanne to go to the horse show to help Jeremy wouldn't do any good. Suzanne didn't like Jeremy very much, either.

But there was something that Suzanne *did* like—showing off.

"It's the perfect place to wear your new cowboy boots," Katie told her. "And that cool black leather cowboy hat you have."

"What about my pink sparkly bandana?" Suzanne added. "It's really pretty."

"Yeah, it is," Katie agreed.

"I don't know," Suzanne said. "I really don't feel like spending a whole afternoon watching Becky."

"Everyone's going to be there," Katie reminded her. "If something happens, you'll be the last to know."

That did it. If there was one thing Suzanne really hated, it was not being the very first person to know something.

"Okay, I'll go," Suzanne said. "It could be a lot of fun. *Especially if Becky messes up.*"

Chapter 7

"There you guys are!" Becky shouted as the kids arrived at the horse show on Saturday afternoon. "You're late. You missed the first event."

"We were waiting for Kevin to get out of karate class," Jessica explained.

"And I had a lawn to rake this morning," Kadeem said. He smiled triumphantly at George.

George smiled back. "So did I," he told Kadeem. "And I have one tomorrow, too."

"Likewise," Kadeem assured him.

"My arms are really tired," George said, "because of all the leaves I raked."

"Not as tired as mine," Kadeem told him.
"And my back hurts, too."

"Yeah, well, my feet—" George began.

"I got second place in my first event," Becky
interrupted the boys in a loud voice. She moved
closer to Jeremy and smiled. "Isn't this the
prettiest ribbon?" she asked him. "I got it for
Showmanship."

Jeremy blushed and turned away.

"I think it's great," Katie complimented her.

She moved in between Jeremy and Becky for a closer look.

Jeremy gave Katie a grateful smile.

"Did you have to jump over fences to win that?" Mandy asked her.

Becky shook her head. "Showmanship is when you lead the pony by the reins. You don't ride him."

Suzanne rolled her eyes. "So you didn't even ride and you got a ribbon?" she asked. "That seems pretty easy."

"It's not," Becky assured her. "I had to groom Brownie. Do you know how long it takes to braid the hair on a horse's mane?"

"I'll bet she's going to tell us," Suzanne whispered to Katie.

Katie poked Suzanne to make her be quiet.

"It took me two hours!" Becky exclaimed.

"See?" Suzanne whispered.

"And that was the easy part," Becky continued. "I worked for weeks to teach Brownie to stand still while the judges graded him on his appearance. And I had to train him to follow a pattern so he could walk in between all these cones they have set up."

"Was he able to do that?" Kevin asked.

Becky nodded. "He did really well."

"Did Brownie get a ribbon, too?" Katie asked her.

Becky looked at Katie strangely. "No. I got the ribbon."

"But Brownie did the work," Katie insisted.

"No, he didn't," Becky insisted. "Why are you making it sound like I did nothing? I trained him. I deserve the ribbon. And I'm going to win another one, too. I have to go get ready for the next event. This time, I'm going to ride Brownie. So there, Katie."

And with that, Becky stomped off.

"Wow, she was mad," George remarked.

"Good one, Katie," Suzanne complimented her.

"Yeah, you told *her*," Jeremy agreed.

But Katie hadn't meant to make Becky

angry. She didn't say Becky didn't deserve *her* ribbon. She just thought Brownie deserved one, too. Katie would never hurt anyone's feelings on purpose.

"I have to go apologize to Becky," Katie told her friends. Becky was probably in the stables with Brownie. She ran off to find her.

★ ★ ★

The horse stables were a big place. Katie didn't see Becky. And after a few minutes of trying to find her, Katie realized she was completely lost. There was nothing around her but hay and empty horse stalls. Rows of them.

Katie sat down on a bale of hay. She looked around, trying to figure out how to get back to the stands. Her friends had surely taken their seats by now.

Suddenly a cool fall breeze began to blow.

Well, it wasn't exactly a *fall* breeze. It was cold, more like something you might feel in winter.

It was also getting pretty strong.

And blowing only on the back of Katie's neck.

Uh-oh. That could only mean one thing.

This was no ordinary wind. This was the *magic wind*!

"No! Not now! Not here!" Katie shouted.

But there was no stopping the magic wind. The tornado whipped around wildly, blowing Katie's bright red hair all around her face.

The magic wind was so strong that Katie was sure she was going to blow up, up, and away—just like a fall leaf. She shut her eyes tight and tried not to cry.

And then it stopped. Just like that.

The magic wind was gone. And so was Katie Kazoo.

She'd turned into someone else . . . switcheroo!

But who?

Chapter 8

Katie blinked twice and slowly opened her eyes. She looked around. There were wooden walls to the left and right of her. If she looked over the half-door in front of her, she could see a horse in a stall across the way.

She must still be in the stables. That was a relief. At least the magic wind hadn't blown her clear across the globe to China or anything.

Okay, so now Katie knew *where* she was. But she still didn't know *who* she was.

Itch. Itch. A fly landed on her back and began walking around. How annoying! Katie swished her tail back and forth, trying to swish off the fly.

Her *tail*? Wait a minute. Katie didn't have a
tail. At least, not usually.

She glanced down at her feet.

Uh-oh. Her funky red high-top sneakers
were gone. She was wearing *horse*shoes instead.
Four horseshoes.

Which could mean only one thing. The
magic wind had switcherooed Katie into a
horse.

Just then, Becky came walking over to the stall. "Hi, Brownie," she said as she petted Katie's long face. "Are you ready for me to ride you?"

Okay, change that. Katie wasn't a horse. She was a pony. *Becky's* pony, Brownie. Any minute now, Becky was going to climb on Katie's back and ride her into the ring.

Only Katie wouldn't know what to do once she got there. She didn't know when to turn left or turn right. She didn't know when to walk slowly or when to gallop.

Katie felt awful. She'd already made Becky feel bad about her red ribbon. And now, if Becky tried to ride her, she would definitely lose this competition.

"Neigh!" Katie whinnied. That was horse language for, "This is sooo not good!"

"What's the matter?" Becky asked Katie. "You sound so sad."

I am sad, Katie thought. *And scared. And kind of hungry, actually.*

Katie walked over to a big pile of hay and began munching on the dry grass. Mmm . . . it was surprisingly good.

"You can't have lunch now, silly," Becky told Katie. "We have to go in the waiting area near the ring." And with that, Becky took Katie's reins and led her out of the stall.

Katie followed Becky as they walked down the narrow hallway between stalls. Finally they reached the waiting area. There were four other ponies with their riders standing beside them. The kids all looked so nice in their black riding helmets, jackets, and boots. The ponies looked nice, too, with their braided manes.

As Katie took her place in the line, Becky suddenly got a weird look on her face. She crossed her legs.

"Oh, no," she said.

Katie cocked her big horse head and looked at her curiously.

"What's the matter, Becky?" a tall girl with a long braid asked.

"I have to go to the bathroom," Becky told her.

"So go," the girl said.

"But I'm supposed to stay with Brownie," Becky said.

"He'll be fine for a few minutes," the girl told her. "We're all here to watch him."

Becky nodded. "Stay here, Brownie," she told Katie.

Katie watched nervously as Becky walked away. This was really scary.

She couldn't think about anything except how Becky was going to try to ride her in front of all those people.

She couldn't think about anything except how all of their friends would make fun of Becky for messing up.

She couldn't think about anything except . . . SUGAR!

Katie smelled something sweet and yummy. A sugar cube was in somebody's pocket. Katie was sure of it.

She raised her horse nose high in the air and

sniffed. The sugary smell was coming from the left.

She sniffed again. Yes. The wonderful smell was coming from a guy working in the stalls nearest the waiting area. He was filling the water trough.

Katie really wanted that sugar. But she knew she was supposed to stay put.

Still, a cube of sugar melting on her tongue would taste sooo good right now. It might even calm her down a little bit.

No. NO! She wasn't supposed to move.

But Katie couldn't help it. She had to have that sugar. Getting around on four legs wasn't something Katie really had the hang of yet. As she tried to turn to the left, she banged into the brown and white pony on her right.

The pony whinnied angrily and kicked Katie's behind.

"Hey," Katie whinnied loudly. "It was an accident."

Katie's whinnying upset two other horses.

One white pony stood up on her hind legs and whinnied loudly.

Katie backed away and banged into another pony, who reared up.

"Powderpuff! Calm down!" a small boy with glasses shouted.

"Down, Chester!" the girl with the long braid cried out. She struggled to keep standing while she held on to her horse's reins.

"Behave, Stardust!" another rider cried to her horse.

Neigh! Neigh! Neigh!

All the horses were whinnying. They'd smelled the sugar. And they wanted it, too!

The man with the sugar cubes in his pocket came walking through the waiting area.

Katie trotted after him.

The other ponies pulled and jumped away from their riders. The kids weren't strong enough to hold on to the reins.

Which meant the ponies were free!

Chapter 9

A moment later, five wild ponies were stampeding into the ring. And Katie was leading them! Woo-hoo!

The sound of the ponies' hooves hitting the dirt was like a drumbeat. Katie was happy to be part of the rhythm.

"Please stop, Brownie!"

Katie turned her head. Becky was running several yards behind the ponies. So were the other kids. But Katie didn't stop. She couldn't. It felt too good to run. She didn't even care about eating the sugar anymore. All Katie wanted to do was gallop as fast as she could.

Clip-clop. Clip-clop.

Katie loved the way the sun felt on her back. And the way her legs stretched out with every stride. Mostly she just loved the freedom of running around the ring. Being cooped up in that little stall all day wasn't any fun.

Okay, so it hadn't been Katie who had been cooped up all day. It had been Brownie. But right now that was the same thing. And whether she was Katie or Brownie, this pony wanted to run!

The fun came to an end when several grown-up horse trainers ran into the ring. As one of them pulled the reins on her bridle, Katie halted, coming to an abrupt stop.

Becky looked horrified!

While the trainer led Katie back to Brownie's stall, she heard kids talking.

"This is all Becky Stern's fault," the girl with the long brown hair said.

"Becky doesn't know anything about training horses," a boy in a black riding helmet added. "She shouldn't have left Brownie alone in the waiting area."

Katie put her head down. Poor Becky. Everyone was blaming her for the pony stampede.

But it wasn't Becky's fault. It was Katie's.

Unfortunately, at the moment, she was the only one who knew that.

* * *

As the door shut on Brownie's stall, Katie went over for a big drink of water. In the distance, she could hear Becky talking to someone. It sounded like Mrs. Stern.

"I'm giving up riding!" Katie heard Becky cry out. "Did you hear what all those kids were saying about me?"

"Becky, this wasn't all your fault," Mrs. Stern told her daughter. "That man shouldn't have had sugar in his pocket when he came near the horses. He told you that. And he said he was sorry."

"But it was Brownie who started misbehaving," Becky insisted. "That means

I didn't train him well enough. And I should never have left him—even to go to the bathroom."

Katie tried to frown. But her horse lips wouldn't turn down that way. Still, she was definitely frowning on the inside. Poor Becky. She had loved horseback riding—until Katie ruined everything.

Just then, Katie felt a cool breeze blowing on her long horse neck. It felt good. She was kind of hot after her run.

But that breeze didn't feel good for long. A moment later it was blowing wildly. In fact, it turned into a tornado. A tornado that was blowing only around Katie.

The magic wind was back!

Katie's horse ears perked up. The whooshing of the wind was really loud now.

It was so strong it could have blown *all* the leaves off a tree in one big whoosh. Katie had never heard anything like it.

Then the noise stopped. So did the tornado.

Just like that. The magic wind was gone.

Katie Carew was back!

Brownie was back, too. The poor little pony seemed very confused.

But there was nothing Katie could do about that. She couldn't even explain the magic wind to her human friends. So what could she possibly say to a pony?

Besides, right now, Katie had to find Becky. She needed to convince her to get right back up on that horse and ride in the competition.

But Katie was going to need help to do that. This was too big a job for just one fourth-grader!

Chapter 10

A few minutes later, Katie and the other kids found Becky standing all by herself behind the stalls. She was crying.

"Becky, there you are," Katie said. She tried to sound cheerful.

"Hi," Becky mumbled. "Um . . . I'm sorry you all came out here for nothing."

"Not for nothing," Katie told her. "We're here to see you ride Brownie."

"I am never getting on that pony again," Becky said. "Or any other horse, either."

"Come on, Becky, you love horseback riding," Emma W. reminded her.

"*Loved*," Becky corrected Emma. "But not

anymore. Didn't you see what happened out there? That whole stampede was my fault."

Katie looked at the ground. Becky's fault? Not exactly.

"You didn't make Brownie run into the ring," Mandy told Becky.

"But I should have been there to control him," Becky said.

"You're just a kid," Kevin told her. "You're still learning."

"So is Brownie," Kadeem pointed out.

"We've all made dumb mistakes," Katie told Becky. "Like the time Mr. G. caught me drawing on my sneakers. It was embarrassing. But I didn't stop drawing."

"And what about when Tony Raven came to town during that big snowstorm?" George reminded her. "He's a professional snowboarder, and he freaked out on that little hill on Surrey Lane *in front of everyone*."

Katie frowned. She knew that wasn't exactly true. *Katie* had been the one to freak out. The magic wind had turned her into Tony Raven that day.

"But he didn't stop snowboarding," George continued. "Last week he won the Snowboard Showdown!"

"And what about my karate tournament?" Kevin remembered. "I tried to break a board with my foot and I fell on my rear end!"

Katie sighed. It hadn't been Kevin who had missed the kick. It had been Katie—thanks to another switcheroo.

"But I went back
and did my next
event. And I got
a medal," Kevin
continued.

"See, Becky?
We all make
mistakes," Katie said.

"Not *all* of us," Suzanne
disagreed.

Kadeem laughed so hard, he almost choked.
"Oh, right. Like you're perfect."

"What about the time you
told everyone that your three-
month-old sister could talk?"
Mandy reminded Suzanne.

Katie sighed again.
That amazing talking
baby? That had been
Katie, too.

"Or the time you put your

63

pants on backward for your modeling show," George remembered.

Now Katie was getting upset. Thanks to the magic wind, she had been on the runway, not Suzanne. Katie had managed to get *all* her friends into messes!

Just then, Jeremy piped up. "One time, when I was six, I kicked the winning soccer goal—into the *other* team's goal cage."

Katie grinned. "And that one wasn't even me!" she exclaimed.

The kids all stared at her.

Oops. "I just meant, that, well . . . never mind," Katie mumbled. "The important thing is that Jeremy went right back to playing soccer."

"And he's the best soccer player in the whole

grade," Becky said. "Maybe even the whole school."

Jeremy blushed.

"Jeremy, do you want me to go back into the ring with Brownie?" Becky asked. "If you want me to, I will."

Say yes, say yes, say yes, Katie thought hopefully, crossing her fingers.

"Whatever," Jeremy mumbled.

Becky brightened. She stood up straight and smiled. "Then I'll do it for you," she told Jeremy. "And I'll win, too!"

Chapter 11

"I can't believe Becky didn't even win a ribbon in that riding competition," Suzanne moaned to Katie on Sunday afternoon. "Especially after we all told her about our embarrassing mistakes!"

Katie rolled her eyes. Suzanne hadn't exactly admitted any mistakes. Everyone else had done that for her.

But out loud Katie said, "I'm just glad she rode Brownie. She only knocked over one cone when she was going through that obstacle course. I think that's pretty good."

Suzanne sat back on the steps of Katie's house. She looked out at the front yard. "Who do you think is making more money?" she asked.

Katie wasn't sure. George was busy raking the leaves at her house. Kadeem was next door, raking Mrs. Derkman's leaves.

"I don't know," Katie said. "George told me he got up early to rake another lawn before ours."

"And Kadeem is raking another lawn after Mrs. Derkman's," Suzanne told Katie. "My next-door neighbor, Mrs. Martin, hired him."

"They're working hard," Katie said. "Look how big that pile is over at Mrs. Derkman's. And ours is pretty huge, too." Because of their leaf-learning adventure in school, Katie now knew there was a maple tree, an oak tree, and two chestnut trees in the Carews' backyard.

"The sooner George is finished, the sooner we can play on your lawn again," Suzanne told her.

"Pepper and Snowball will be happy about that," Katie said. She looked over toward where Pepper and Mrs. Derkman's dog were resting. "I'll bet they're pretty bored just lying there under that maple."

Suzanne looked over at the two dogs. "They seem pretty happy to me," she said. "Dogs are lazy, anyway."

"They are not," Katie insisted. She hated when anyone—even her best friend—said anything bad about Pepper. Or *his* best friend, Snowball, either.

Just then, a little gray squirrel raced across Mrs. Derkman's lawn. Immediately Pepper and Snowball jumped up and—*whoosh*—they took off.

"Pepper! No!" Katie shouted. "Snowball, stop!"

But it was too late. The next thing anyone knew, Pepper and Snowball had plowed right into Kadeem's giant pile of leaves. Red, orange, and yellow leaves flew all over Mrs. Derkman's lawn.

But instead of yelling at the dogs, Kadeem stormed over to George.

"This is all your fault!" Kadeem shouted.

"*My* fault?" George asked. "What did I do?"

"You sent those dogs over to Mrs. Derkman's lawn!" Kadeem insisted.

"No way," George said. "But now you're going to have to rake up all those leaves again. Maybe *I'll* go over and rake Mrs. Martin's lawn. You're not going to have time now."

"You wouldn't dare!" Kadeem shouted.

"Oh, wouldn't I?" George shouted back.

Kadeem jumped up and took a flying leap—

right into George's pile of leaves. Red, orange, and yellow leaves flew all over Katie's lawn.

Now it was George's turn to get mad. He

ran over to Mrs. Derkman's lawn and began throwing leaves all over the place.

Kadeem did the same thing on Katie's lawn.

George ran over to Kadeem and dumped a whole pile of leaves on his head.

"I'll get you for that, George Brennan!" Kadeem shouted. He picked up his own pile of leaves.

"This is really getting bad!" Katie told Suzanne. "We have to do something."

"No, we don't," Suzanne said. "I think it's hilarious. Better than anything on TV!"

But Katie was tired of all the fighting. She ran over and stood between the boys.

"STOP!" she shouted.

The boys didn't hear her. They were too busy throwing leaves.

"Ptttthhhht . . ." Katie mumbled as a handful of dried leaves landed in her mouth.

"Oops," George said. "Kadeem did that."

"I did not," Kadeem insisted. "Those were George's leaves."

"I don't care whose leaves they were!" Katie shouted as she picked bits of dried leaves off her tongue. "I just want you guys to cut it out." She looked at both yards. What a mess!

"George should pick up my leaves," Kadeem started in again.

"*He* should pick up mine," George corrected him.

"No! You're both going to help each other!" Katie told them.

"Why would we do that?" George and Kadeem asked at the same time.

"Because it'll go a lot faster," Katie told the boys. "In fact, if you guys worked together all the time, you'd probably both make a lot more money."

Kadeem and George just stared at each other.

Finally George said, "We could rake five or six lawns a day that way."

"I can only do two a day on my own," Kadeem admitted.

"George and Kadeem's Leaf-Busting

Business," George said. "I like that."

"You mean, *Kadeem* and George's Leaf-Busting Business," Kadeem said.

Katie frowned. She could sense another fight coming on.

"What about just calling it Leaf Busters?" she suggested.

George and Kadeem both smiled. They liked the sound of that.

"Right now, you'd better rake up this mess," Katie told the boys. "Start with Mrs. Derkman's lawn. She'll be really mad if she sees it like this."

George and Kadeem didn't have to be told twice. They both knew Mrs. Derkman well.

Besides being Katie's neighbor, she was the strictest teacher in the whole school.

And boy, could she yell.

"Hey, Katie, you want to go inside and listen to a Bayside Boys CD?" Suzanne called out.

For a minute, Katie thought about staying outside and helping the boys. But they seemed to be working really well on their own.

"Sure!" Katie shouted back at Suzanne. She turned toward her house. But before she could take even one step, a cool breeze began to blow on her neck.

Katie gasped.

Oh, no! Was the magic wind back? Was it going to switcheroo her again? Right here? In front of her friends?

Just then, Katie noticed the trees were moving with the wind. And so was the flag outside Mrs. Derkman's house.

Phew. This wasn't the magic wind at all. It was just a regular old fall wind.

Katie was sooo glad. She was really happy to be Katie Carew, ordinary fourth-grader.

At least for now.

Don't *Leaf* Just Yet!

Mr. G. had a lot of extra leaves left over once the kids had finished decorating their beanbags (and themselves!). But he didn't let them go to waste. Katie's mega-cool teacher showed the kids how to make autumn leaf prints. Then he hung their artwork all over class 4A.

Here's how you can make leaf print pictures of your own! Hang them in your classroom or your bedroom. It's a great way to keep the fun fall spirit going all year long!

You will need: fresh, moist, colorful autumn leaves (try choosing leaves that are all different colors and shapes), a thick wooden board, thumbtacks, unbleached muslin material, glue, scissors, a hammer, and a brown paper grocery bag. You'll also need a grown-up to help you with the tacks and the hammering.

Here's what you do:

1. Gather your fresh, moist, colorful leaves and place them in the grocery bag.

2. Cut your muslin material into a 12-inch-by-12-inch square.

3. Place one leaf on the wooden board.

4. Cover the leaf with the muslin. Have a grown-up help you tack the muslin to the board so it won't move.

5. Use your hammer to beat on the part of the muslin that is covering the leaf. (Be sure a grown-up is around while you do this and make sure to hit every part of the leaf. That's how

you make sure all the color comes off onto the muslin material.)

6. Continue to place one leaf at a time under your muslin material and hammer each one completely. The colors of the leaves will come off onto your material.

7. When you are finished making your print, brush off any leaf parts left on the material.

8. Create a frame from black or brown construction paper and glue your leaf print to the paper frame.

9. Hang your artwork on your wall. But tape it up well. You don't want your leaf print to *fall!*

About the Author

Nancy Krulik is the author of more than 150 books for children and young adults, including three *New York Times* best sellers. She lives in New York City with her husband, composer Daniel Burwasser, and their children, Amanda and Ian. When she's not busy writing the Katie Kazoo, Switcheroo series, Nancy loves swimming, reading, and going to the movies.

About the Illustrators

John & Wendy have illustrated all of the Katie Kazoo books, but when they're not busy drawing Katie and her friends, they like to paint, take photographs, travel, and play music in their rock 'n' roll band. They live and work in Brooklyn, New York.